W9-CPE-969

# Doodle with Dora!

**A GOLDEN BOOK • NEW YORK**

ISBN: 978-0-375-86602-9

www.randomhouse.com/kids

Printed in the United States of America

10 9 8 7 6 5 4 3

¡*Hola!* I'm Dora.
What's your name? Will you write it here?

Are you ready for a drawing adventure?
All the pictures in this book need
to be finished. Will you help? Great!

# Will you finish the swing so that I can play on it?

# Will you finish the swing for Boots?

# Let's ride the seesaw!

Will you draw a sidewalk for me to skate on?

# I love basketball. Where's the basket?

# What am I jumping over?

# Will you draw a balloon for Boots?

# Will you draw two balloons for me?

# I'm looking for ladybugs.
## Will you draw some?

# I'd like to give this yummy nut to a squirrel.

# Will you draw a frog for me to hop with?

**Let's add more flowers to my garland.**

I wish I had more leaves to play in.

Let's pick apples.
Will you draw more on the branch?

Will you draw some wheels so that
I can ride my bike?

# Will you draw some wheels on Boots's bike?

I want to take my puppy for a walk.
Will you draw a leash?

# My puppy needs a doghouse.
## Will you draw one?

I think my puppy needs
another puppy to play with.

# Isa loves soccer. Give her a ball!

# Go, team! Dora is cheering the team on. Will you draw team flags?

# Will you draw team flags for Boots?

# I can spin the ball on my finger.

# I'm winning the race!
## Will you draw a ribbon for me to break?

# I won a medal!

Where's my soccer ball?
Will you draw one for me?

 **Do you see a sunny sky or a rainy day?**

Boots and I are having a picnic.
Will you draw us a blanket?

# Let's pick strawberries.
## Will you fill this bush with berries?

# Will you draw a string for my kite?

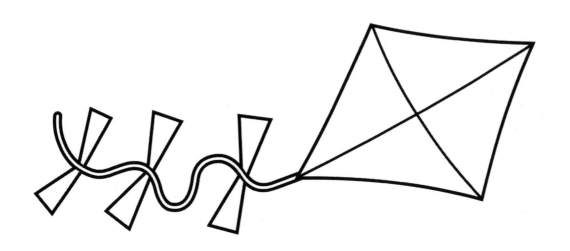

Boots wants a really long tail on his kite.
Will you help him out?

# Who's in the nest?

 We need a vine to swing on. Will you help us?

Oh, no! There's an alligator on the bridge.
Will you draw another bridge for us to cross?

Let's have a circus adventure.
Will you draw a big tent?

Boots needs a tightrope to walk across.

# Will you give me a sweet circus treat?

 **Benny needs a few scoops of ice cream.**

# Draw two balloons so that Tico can fly up, up, and away!

Boots needs a baton so that
he can lead the circus parade.

# Draw yourself in a silly costume.

I need a hat to be a real
rootin', tootin' cowgirl.

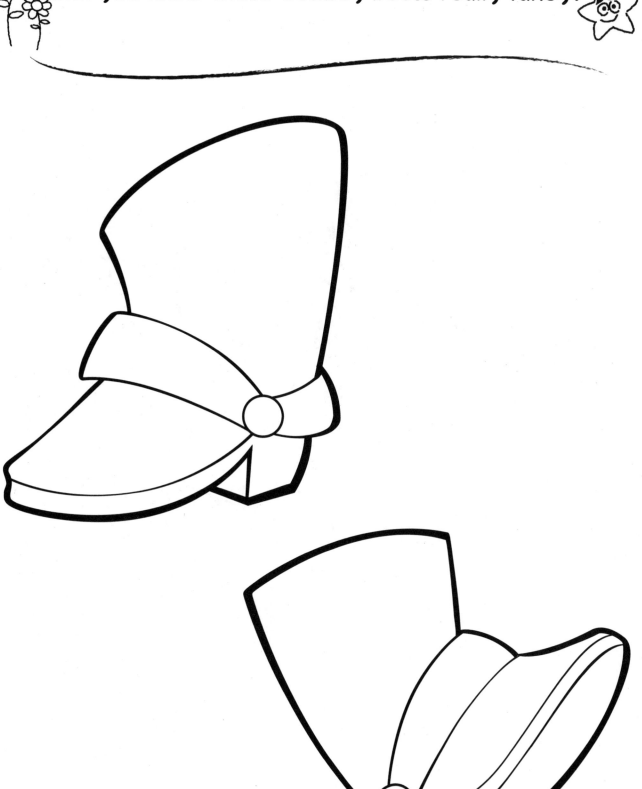

 Will you draw a road for Tico to drive on?

# Will you draw a stop sign?

# We need a piñata for our fiesta!

# Help us fill the air with bubbles!

# Draw a cake for the fiesta.

# How many cookies did Boots bake?

# Will you make a silly fiesta hat for me?

# Boots needs a silly hat, too!

 **Will you give Tico something to juggle?**

# Will you draw some water for our canoe?

# Boots's sailboat needs a sail!

# How many fish does Boots see?

# Will you draw a surfboard for me?

# Draw a big wave for Swiper.

# Will you draw a diving board for me?

We like to make footprints in the mud!

# Boots needs his boots!

**We're building a sand castle. Will you help?**

# Let's play catch.
## We need a big, colorful beach ball!

# Raise the sail on this pirate ship.

 **This pirate piggy needs his captain's hat.**

# Let's clean up this beach. Help us by circling the things that belong in the trash.

Look! There's a surprise inside the giant clam.

**Will you draw another dolphin jumping out of the water?**

# Here comes Mariana the Mermaid Princess.
## Will you draw her castle?

# Make this crown really fancy!

This magical crown has turned me into a mermaid! Will you draw my tail?

 **This unicorn has lost his horn! Will you help him?**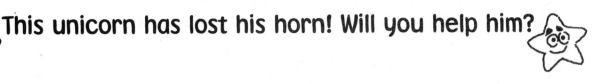

© Viacom International Inc.

Will you decorate my royal gown?

# We're flying on our friend Pegasus. Will you draw a rainbow?

# Where are my magical fairy wings?

# Boots needs fairy wings, too!

# I'm in the Snow Princess's tower.
## Will you finish the walls?

# This king needs a crown.

# Will you design a beautiful dress for me?

I wish I could be a princess
with a beautiful tiara.

# Will you decorate my tutu?

# Swiper needs a fancy hat.

# What does your tutu look like?
## Draw yourself dancing in it.

Will you draw a fancy bow tie for Boots?

I love the pretty flower on my dress.
I wish I had one in my hair, too.

Flowers make me happy.
Will you draw my smile?

# Will you draw some water to make my flower grow?

# Use the key to color these flowers for Isa.

| KEY |
| --- |
| 1 = Green  2 = Yellow  3 = Red  4 = Blue |

# Will you draw Isa's flower basket?

# Who's that flying over me?

Tico's scooter needs wheels
so that he can go fast. *¡Rapido, Tico!*

# Will you finish this picture of Backpack by adding a big smile?

# This train needs some tracks!

# Let's go hiking.
## Will you make it a beautiful sunny day?

I love to camp out.
Will you set up my tent?

# Will you help me draw my sleeping bag?

Boots and I are going into space.
But first, Boots needs a helmet.

# Will you draw us a rocket?

 I don't want to get lost in space. Will you draw a line to connect me to the rocket?

# Will you help Boots put a flag on the moon?

# Draw hands on the clock
# to show what time it is.

# Boots needs help finishing his snowman.

# Will you fill this ice cave with icicles?

# Will you finish this picture of Map by adding a big smile?

# Will you draw a road to connect all the places on the map?

I found a little star.
Draw three more stars to keep him company.

We're having a birthday party for Boots.
Will you draw hats for everyone?

# Let's make a banana cake for Boots.

# Help Tico and Isa decorate the banner for the party.

# Will you decorate my card for Boots?

# Will you decorate these gifts for Boots?

# Boots loves bananas.
## Will you draw two more for him?

# Benny needs six strings on his guitar.

# What is Swiper swiping?

**Draw Swiper on this poster.**

# Help! I need a bridge to get to Boots.

# We want to come to your house.
## Will you draw it for us?

I want to go up to see Boots.
Will you draw some stairs?

# Will you make a frame for my painting?

# Will you draw some toys for my little brother and sister?

# Abuela loves flowers.
# Will you draw some for her?

I love my teddy bear.
Will you draw your favorite toy?

# Sweet dreams, Boots.
## Will you add some stars to the sky?

**Thank you for doodling with me.**
*¡Hasta luego!* **See you later!**